# TROLL TALES

Translation: Pat Shaw

Illustrations: Rolf Lidberg
Text: Jan Lööf

CAPPELEN DAMM

«Now we're going to have a history lesson,» said Great Grandfather, and took out his history book.

«We don't want to hear any old history,» cried all the troll children. «Can't you make up something new?»

«No, I can't,» said Great Grandfather. «But I can tell about some present-day history. About things that took place a short time ago. They're not in this book, but I'll try to remember what happened recently.»

«Let me think,» said Great Grandfather. «What happened last year? Oh yes, there was that trouble at Easter time. Do you remember?»

«No, we've forgotten,» said the troll children. «Tell us about it.»

«Well, the hens over at Troll Farm got so angry when the children started gathering eggs. 'Don't take all the eggs!' squawked one of the hens. 'Then we won't have any baby chicks!'

But no one understood what she said, because when a hen speaks it only sounds like *'Cackle cackle!'*»

«I was there and painted Easter eggs myself,» said Great Grandfather. «I think it's fun. But, as I said, the hens got angry. And then the trouble really began when Mattias smashed an egg on his little brother's head. All the children started throwing eggs at each other. The hens started squawking at the top of their lungs, and the rooster ran about flapping his wings and was frightened out of his wits. Easter got off to a bad start. Although it was clear that we also had a little fun.»

Now it was summer. Around the beginning of June Little Per and I were out walking in the fields. We'd forgotten that the elk cows had just calved. Then they're very bad-tempered. An elk cow came rushing towards us, and we had to hide among the bushes. But we peeped out as quietly as we could, because we wanted to have a look at the calf. It was so nice and had a light brown coat.

After midsummer it was time to mow and take in the hay. I had my old scythe and thought I'd help out. But I've grown a bit lazy in my old age, and when I saw Lill Fia come running along I called her. I told her I was thinking of sneaking away from the work, and she thought this was a good idea. So we played all day, instead.

Even though we were lazy, the others worked all the harder. Troll Oscar, who lives up on the hill, had risen early in order to help with the haymaking. But his old scythe was blunt and rusty, and couldn't be used.

«How will I ever manage to sharpen the scythe all by myself?» he muttered.

Just then Björne and little Ida came along.

«We can help you,» they said, and started to turn the handle so that Oscar could grind the blade.

Everyone worked hard and helped in the hayfield. I didn't think they would notice that I wasn't there. But Maja-Stina, who brought coffee and buns, told on me to the others:

«I saw Great Grandfather and Lill Fia playing up at the mountain farm,» she said. Troll Oscar roared with laughter.

«As soon as there's work to be done, he sneaks away,» Oscar chuckled.

Oh, how ashamed I was afterwards!

The days went by and summer soon came to an end.

One beautiful autumn day someone could be heard shouting, «The cloudberries are ripe out on the marsh!»

Lingonberries and blueberries grow everywhere. But cloudberries are harder to find and only grow in special places. So it pays to keep one's eye's peeled. Sometimes hordes of Norwegian trolls come and pick all the berries in a few hours. But last year Great Grandfather got there first, and gave everyone who lived in Troll Valley as many cloudberries as they wanted.

I never eat berries myself. I only like boiled potatoes. But I've been wandering in the fields all my life, so I know exactly where the berries grow.

I can find every strawberry patch for miles around. I guess that's why I'm so popular with you youngsters, isn't it? When you go on an outing with me, you know you're going to find strawberries.

I also know where to find lots of lingonberries, and I usually help the Troll wives to pick them. They need plenty of lingonberries in order to make jam.

Picking berries is easy, but cleaning them is hard work. So I've built a cleaning contraption. The contraption works very well, but my arm aches a bit after I sit and turn the handle all day.

Last autumn was dark and gloomy, but we took out our instruments in order to cheer ourselves up with some music. Gunnar Bergsen, over in the scree, is a whizz at playing the saw. Especially in a minor key. And his favourite melody is *When Mama Troll Puts Her Eleven Troll Babies to Bed.*

When he moves the bow across the saw, the mood he creates is incredible. Everyone seems to be under a spell.

On Saturday evenings music could be heard everywhere in Troll Valley. If one took a walk up on the mountain, when the weather was fine and the air was still, one could clearly hear accordion music down in the valley. And not only accordions but also fiddles, clarinets, singing and laughter. From another mountain top in the distance one might also hear the notes of a birch-bark lur.

One blows a birch-bark lur in exactly the same way as one blows a trumpet. The notes can be heard for miles around, and messages may be sent back and forth from great distances.

One Saturday night the Trulsson family had climbed up on Copper Hill. From there they could see a huge bonfire over on Lapplander Mountain. And Mrs. Trulsson, who is curious, blew a signal on her lur.

That evening Lapplander Mountain was crowded with trolls. Even though they were making lots of noise, the signal from Copper Hill could be heard clearly.

Jocke had brought along his birch-bark lur, and he blew four notes in reply. This meant, «We're having a party! Come on over!»

And what a party it was! All the trolls in Troll Valley came. And we sang and played and told stories until the wee hours of the morning.